COMPROMISED BRIDE GEORGIA

Compromised Brides series

Cheryl Wright

Copyright

Georgia
(Compromised Brides series)

Copyright ©2022 by Cheryl Wright

Dedication

To Margaret Tanner, my very dear friend and fellow author, for her enduring encouragement and friendship.

To Alan, my husband of over forty-nine years, who has been a relentless supporter of my writing and dreams for many years.

To You, my wonderful readers, who encourage me to continue writing these stories. It is such a joy knowing so many of you enjoy reading my stories as much as I love writing them for you.

Table of Contents

Dedication 3

Table of Contents 4

Chapter One.. 5

Chapter Two 9

Chapter Three... 20

Chapter Four.. 31

Chapter Five 42

Chapter Six.. 50

Chapter Seven 59

Chapter Eight... 71

Chapter Nine 80

Chapter Ten 88

Epilogue 99

From the Author 107

About the Author...................................... 108

Links.. 109

Chapter One

Pine Creek, Montana – 1880's

Georgia Rose had objected to the party from the moment Mother told her about it.

They were not rich folk, and didn't have to attend every party like high society. But Mother insisted. It was high time she married, according to all Mother's friends, so the pressure was on. Not that Georgia had any intention of marrying. She was happy being a spinster.

She was happy in her position of schoolmarm, and would continue that for many years, given the opportunity. There was only one reason she had gone along to the party — to make her mother happy.

"Hurry up and mingle," Mother hissed. "You're doing yourself no favors."

Georgia rolled her eyes. This was more a party for the ordinary folk like them, not the rich and famous. Why her mother thought she would snag a husband here, Georgia did not know. She sipped her lemonade and decided to make the best of an unpleasant situation. Relaxing for the first time, she chatted with the other women sitting on the sidelines as they enjoyed the music.

"Excuse me, Miss Rose." The voice was vaguely familiar, and Georgia turned to face him. *Sherman Ryan!* He had been pursuing her for as long as Georgia could remember. Mother could never understand why she abhorred the man, who had an unsavory reputation. She screwed up her nose. "May I have this dance?"

Mother nudged her in the ribs. "Of course you may," her mother answered on Georgia's behalf. "My daughter came here to dance, after all."

Whether Scarlet Rose was aware of Sherman's reputation or not, it was not Mother's place to accept his offer in her place. "No, Mother!" she snapped. "I don't want to dance with him."

Scarlet merely smiled at Sherman, then put a hand to Georgia's back. "She's a little shy," she told the man, which was far from the truth. If it had been anyone but him, Georgia would have gladly danced. But not with this awful man.

Now she had no choice.

Sherman's hand held hers, and he pulled Georgia to her feet. He tried to draw her close, but Georgia ensured she kept her distance. The music soon mesmerized her, and it wasn't until it became faint to her ears she realized they had danced their way out into the garden.

They were completely alone.

She glanced up into Sherman's face, and the grin he wore terrified her. One hand grabbed at her bottom, and the other went to her breast. Before she could step out of his reach, an arm went up her back, pulling her close to him. Sherman kissed her as he squeezed her breast, then his mouth moved down to her neck.

Georgia screamed long and loud, even as she fought to remove his hand from her breast. The party goers came running. She realized too late her scream had let everyone know this revolting man had compromised her. She had no other choice but to leave town.

It had pained Georgia to pack up her belongings from the schoolhouse more than it had from home. Her clothes and other belongings had no emotional impact for her, but as she glanced around the school for the last time, she knew it would be difficult to leave. Thank goodness the children weren't there. Little did they know tomorrow would bring them a brand new teacher. Someone who had been eager to take her place as school teacher for a very long time.

It was all behind her now, and the best she could do for herself was to move on. Scarlet, her mother, couldn't believe what had happened. Blissfully unaware of Sherman's past behavior, she'd seen him as a potential father to Georgia's future children. All that despite her declaration of not wanting a husband, let alone children.

Why everyone pressured women into marrying and producing a family, she didn't know. They didn't stop to think it was mostly women who made up the teacher circle. With every woman producing children, who did they think would teach their children? Obviously thought was beyond the majority. She shook her head. This was hard enough without trying to work out the motives of others.

She packed the last of her personal possessions and took a long look around the room. Georgia knew this would be the last time she ever set foot inside the building. Probably also the last time she was in her hometown. Where she would go, or what she would do now, she didn't know. Her mind was in turmoil.

Tomorrow morning, she would take the stagecoach out of town to a place far away. Somewhere she wasn't known and her tarnished reputation wouldn't follow her. She stepped outside and locked the door for the very last time.

Chapter Two

Outside Pleasant Grove, Montana – 1880's

"Ready yourselves, boys!"

Georgia heard the words of the stagecoach driver, but did not know what was going on. "Brace yourself, Miss Rose," the old cowboy sitting opposite her said. "It's a robbery." He reached into his jacket and pulled out a pistol, much to Georgia's surprise.

"Oh!" It was all she could get out. Shock had taken over. She now wished she'd changed to the train at the last stop. It would have been far more comfortable, but with only two more stops to go, she didn't think it was worth the hassle.

"Lay down on the floor," he bellowed as gunfire rang out. "Don't want you being hit." She hurried to lie down, despite her reluctance. How long had it been since they cleaned the floor? It was putrid. The smell alone was enough to stop her from getting down. Suddenly she was shoved lower. A hand to her back ensured it had happened.

How rude, she thought, but knew the cowboy was only trying to help. Instead of saying something, she prayed. Not only for herself, but for everyone on the stagecoach. They were all at risk. All would mostly likely die in the next few minutes.

"You need to stay down," he hissed. "It's going to get nasty, I can feel it." Next thing she knew, the old man was hit. "Urgh!" he yelled, then slumped down in his seat.

Her first instinct was to scream. But if they didn't know she was there, it would be far safer. Georgia lifted her head slightly, trying to see how the driver and guards were doing. The three men were slumped in their seats. Who was driving the stagecoach if they weren't?

Out of the blue, gunfire began again. This time, even closer. Her heart pounded, and sweat poured from her brow. If the robbers found her, they wouldn't let her live. The last thing they would want was a witness. She was the sole survivor. At least until this moment. Was this the end?

"Whoa!" She heard the unfamiliar voice as the horses were pulled to a halt. Apart from his voice trying to slow the horses, the silence was palpable. The air was full of dust, and her head pounded with worry. Soon she would be murdered and her mother would never know what happened to her.

Not only had she been disgraced in front of the entire town, she was about to be obliterated from this earth. Never to be heard of again.

Her first reaction was to run. But where would she run to? She didn't know the area, and more than likely, it was barren. Even with a few trees jotted about, she wouldn't stay hidden for long. The robbers would find her. If they didn't kill her, they'd claim her as their own, and that would be worse than death.

Her heart pounded at her impending murder, and Georgia felt lightheaded. All because Sherman Ryan couldn't keep his hands to himself.

Low mutterings outside alerted her to the fact they'd come closer to the stagecoach. They were, in fact, right outside the door. Suddenly, the door opened and a large man stood in the doorway looking down at her. She huddled into a ball on the floor, but there was no way to hide. He had the doorway obstructed, so she couldn't run. Nor would she want to. A bullet to the back of the head was not the way she wanted to leave this world.

"Ma'am," the voice said. He outstretched a hand. She moved further away. "Ma'am," he said again, more gently this time. "It's alright. You're safe. The robbers are all dead."

Georgia wasn't sure if she should believe him, but what choice did she have? As far as she could tell, he was one of them. One of the robbers.

"Ma'am," he said again. "I am Sheriff Drake Calhoun. It's safe to come outside." His hand touched hers. "Keep your eyes closed – it's not a pretty sight. I'll guide you out."

Despite the shudders that wracked her entire body, Georgia somehow managed to climb off the floor and out of the carriage. Disregarding the sheriff's words, she glanced about at the carnage. Her eyes then fell on the aging cowboy who had saved her life. Great sobs wracked her body, and the sheriff pulled her close against him. It was the first act of kindness she'd encountered for a very long time.

"I feel so embarrassed," Georgia said as she sat opposite the sheriff. She glanced about his office. It was what she expected. There were two desks, one for him, and one for his deputy. A chair sat on either side of each desk, and there was a large cupboard. Presumably, they kept the files in there.

"Nothing to feel embarrassed about," Sheriff Calhoun said firmly. "You handled it better than most women would have."

She sighed. She would have preferred not to handle it at all. If the robbers had left them alone, none of this would have happened. "That cowboy, Rory, he saved my life."

The sheriff studied her. "I'm sorry about Rory. He was a good man." She could see the pain on his face.

"You knew him?"

"He lived here in Pleasant Grove. On one of the ranches." He ran a hand through his hair, then picked up his pencil again. "I need some details. Miss Rose. What is your occupation?" He stared at her curiously. Georgia was intensely aware most women married and didn't have any work experience as a result.

"I'm a schoolteacher," she said firmly.

The sheriff dropped his pencil. "A schoolteacher? We need one of those here in town. The children have been without a teacher for a very long time." He seemed to measure his next words. "No one wants to come all the way out here."

"Because of robbers?"

He nodded then. "Sad but true," he finally said. "Where were you headed? I'm sure it wouldn't have been here."

That was a question she didn't have an answer to. Georgia licked her lips. "I… well, I honestly can't say I know."

He stared at her then, a frown forming. "On a trip to nowhere." He chuckled then, as though he found the thought funny. "Well, I guess we need to find somewhere for you to stay. We have two options, the saloon, which I don't recommend, or Miss Jenny's Boarding House. Oh, and we were able to retrieve your luggage." He indicated her trunk in a far corner. "It bears a dent or two from flying bullets. Hopefully, there's no damage inside." When he stood Georgia followed his lead.

"Miss Jenny's sounds good. Hopefully, she has a room available." Georgia straightened her skirts.

The sheriff chuckled again. "She will. We don't get a lot of travelers out here. Not even when the stage comes through. Those fool robbers must have thought there was gold on the stage. Why they would think that, I'll never know." He walked over to the door and opened it, ushering her through. Presumably they would retrieve her trunk later, when she'd settled in. "Miss Jenny's isn't far," he said.

Georgia glanced up at *Miss Jenny's Boarding House for Discerning Women*. It looked homely and welcoming from the outside. The white picket fence hid the well cared for garden until you were upon it. There was a cobblestone path leading up to the front door. Through the windows, you could see the ruffled curtains, and she could only imagine what it was like inside. Her eyes went higher to see there was another level to the building. She could only imagine this would have been a bustling town in its heyday.

"It looks lovely," she said in delight. It took all her might not to clap her hands.

The sheriff opened the picket gate and ushered her ahead, then knocked on the door. It wasn't long before it was opened. "Morning, Miss Jenny. This is Miss Georgia Rose," he said. "She needs a room."

Miss Jenny studied her for only a moment. "You weren't on the stage when…" She took a deep breath. "My dear girl, come inside. You too, Sheriff. The kettle is boiling." She led them into a cozy entrance, then took them through the sitting room to the kitchen. The aroma coming from that room was enticing, and Georgia was certain she would be happy here.

Not that she'd planned on staying long. She'd had such an awful experience here, she would leave as soon as she could. If she had the choice, she would never step foot on a stagecoach again. She sighed. That was probably the only mode of transport out of this backwater.

"Do sit yourselves down," Miss Jenny said. "Tea or coffee, Miss Rose?"

"Tea please. And call me Georgia. My students call me Miss Rose."

The older woman lifted an eyebrow. "You're a teacher?" She smiled and glanced across at the sheriff. "Did you know about this?"

"Just found out," he said, then sipped the coffee Miss Jenny placed in front of him.

"How long do you plan on staying, Georgia?" Their host sat a plate full of cake slices between them all, then sat down with her own cup of tea. "Because we desperately need a school teacher here."

"The sheriff told me, but I have no plans to stay beyond a day or two. Long enough to recover from the shock."

"We lost Rory today," Sheriff Calhoun said quietly, his eyes on Miss Jenny.

She straightened her shoulders. "I heard. It's a tragedy. He might have been rough around the edges, but Rory was a gentleman and would do anything for anyone."

Georgia swallowed down the emotion that hit her once again. "He saved my life," she whispered.

"That was Rory. We need to give him the send-off he deserves." Miss Jenny wiped at her eyes.

It was clear these people had a lot of time for the old cowboy. They may even have loved him. Rory died because of her. "I'm sorry," Georgia said. "It's my fault. He died because he was protecting me." Tears pooled in her eyes, but she wouldn't let them fall, and battered her eyes trying to fight them off. Drake Calhoun passed her his handkerchief.

"It is not your fault," he said gently. "Rory was protecting himself as well. If you weren't there, he wouldn't have done anything differently. Of that, I'm certain."

She nodded as she wiped at her eyes, but wasn't convinced. She would hang around long enough to honor the old cowboy at his funeral, then she would leave. It was the least she could do for the man who had saved her life. "When will the funeral be, Sheriff?" Georgia asked. "And when is the next stagecoach out of town?"

"Not sure about the funeral, tomorrow maybe. Day after. I'll let you know." He drained his mug of the coffee before answering the rest of her question. "Stage comes through but once a week. So this time next week."

She was stuck here for an entire week? It took all her effort not to groan. Instead, she nodded. "I guess you have me for a week, Miss Jenny." She smiled then. It was the last thing she felt like doing, but her hostess had been nothing but kind.

"I'm sure you'll enjoy your stay in Pleasant Grove," she said. "And please, call me Jenny." The older woman stood then. "Let me show you to your room. It's not huge, but it's clean and comfortable. There are three other ladies staying here, but they're at work right now. You'll meet them tonight."

"I'll leave you to it," the sheriff said. "I'll bring your trunk over shortly." He snatched up another piece of cake with a grin, then turned to leave.

"Join us for supper, Sheriff?" Jenny called to his retreating back.

He appeared surprised as he turned to face her. "Thank you, I'd love to. See you then." He left them alone then.

"Follow me," Jenny said, then led her out of the kitchen and upstairs. "This will be your room." She unlocked the door, then opened it wide.

Georgia gasped. The room was beautifully decorated. The furniture was sparse – there was a bed, a side table and a small closet. In the far corner stood a comfortable chair. The window overlooked a hillside, and the view was stunning. As she'd seen from outside, the curtains were pretty. They were made from a sheer white material and had been perfectly ruffled along the edges. Matching ribbons held them back during the day.

She turned to face Jenny. "It's beautiful," she said, then sat on the edge of the bed, giving a tiny bounce. "The bed seems comfortable, too." She smiled then. Probably the first time since the attack earlier in the day.

"I'm pleased you like it. Meals are included in the price." She quoted a price that seemed very reasonable to Georgia, and she reached into her reticule and paid. Not that Jenny would have demanded it, but she felt better knowing her week's rent was settled. "Why don't you rest? You've been through a terrible experience. A nap would do you good." She left the room then, closing the door behind her.

Georgia glanced about. She liked it here in this town. So far, people had been lovely. And kind. Despite her experience earlier today, she didn't hate this place. It wasn't the fault of the town, and it wasn't her fault. She had no choice but to stay for an entire week, but then she would leave. Getting on the next stagecoach would be difficult, but if she wanted to leave, and she did, then Georgia had to bite the bullet and do it.

Chapter Three

Sheriff Drake Calhoun finished filling out all the paperwork just in time for supper at Miss Jenny's. She occasionally invited him, knowing he was single and didn't eat well otherwise. He often had invitations from the townsfolk, and he appreciated them all. But he savored Miss Jenny's invites more than the other because she was such an excellent cook.

He felt certain the older woman was trying to match him up with one of her boarders. Which one, he didn't know, but it hadn't worked. He was happily single and wanted to stay that way. Besides, with all the supper invitations he received, why did he need a wife?

The life of a sheriff was a dangerous one, and it was not something he wanted to contemplate. If he married and was killed in the line of duty, what would happen to his wife? She would be homeless, as the next sheriff would need their cottage, plus she would be left to fend for herself.

No, this was far better. It also protected his heart. "I'm off," he called to his deputy, who was delivering food to their one prisoner – a drunkard who became too boisterous for the other saloon customers. Once he sobered up, they'd send him on his way.

Clyde Lawson, his deputy, suddenly appeared. "Enjoy," he said. "I'm sure you will. I never get invitations to Miss Jenny's, more's the pity."

"Being sheriff has its perks." Drake shrugged his shoulders then.

"You're correct there," the Clyde said. "More money, plus fed by the best cooks." He smiled then, alerting Drake to the fact he was joking.

He left the sheriff's office and headed to Miss Jenny's. The town was quiet except for a few people going home from work. The mercantile suddenly went dark, and he knew the owners would go out the back to their home and have a meal. The bank manager was locking up, and the dressmaker was leaving her store too.

It all meant he was late.

He hurried to the boarding house and knocked on the door. "My apologies," he told Jenny when she opened it. "Paperwork," he said, then shrugged his shoulders.

"I was worried you weren't coming," she said. "I've made one of your favorite meals, too." He followed her into the kitchen, where the four boarders sat around the wooden table.

"Evening, ladies," he said, pulling his hat from his head. They all smiled at him and returned his greeting. Except for Georgia Rose. She looked downright sad. Not that he could blame her. The woman had been through hell and back.

"Sit yourself down next to Georgia." Jenny was firm in her instruction, and Drake had no intention of crossing the woman. He only hoped she wasn't trying to hook him up with yet another of her boarders. Besides, she was leaving on the next stage in precisely one week. "Miss Rose," he said as he sat.

She threw him a fleeting smile. "Georgia please." She reached for her water and took a dainty sip. A shiver went down his spine watching her. Drake slapped himself mentally. What was wrong with him? Women did not interest him, especially those who already declared they were leaving town in one week.

"There you are, Sheriff," Jenny said, as she placed the large platter in the center of the table.

"Smells amazing, as always." He leaned forward to take in the full experience. Roast chicken with roasted vegetables and gravy. Once Jenny sat, they joined hands for grace. Drake held Georgia's soft hand. It felt so tiny inside his hand. His first instinct was to rub his thumb against her gentle skin, but that seemed so intimate.

She glanced down at their entwined hands and smiled. This time it wasn't so brief, and warmth spread through him. It was as though that smile was meant only for him, but Drake doubted it. He reluctantly closed his eyes.

"Dear Lord," Jenny said, "please bless this food, and the people at this table. Amen."

He opened his eyes and glanced around the table. It was bad manners to eat before the ladies. He leaned forward and lifted the platter, offering the meal first to Jenny, then Georgia. He made his way around the table, ensuring all the women had their share before he did. Last of all, he added the gravy. Miss Jenny's gravy was the best he'd ever eaten, and that included his own mother's.

"Tuck in, everyone," Jenny said. "Don't wait for it to get cold."

"Where are you from?" Mary, one of the other boarders, asked.

"Pine Creek. If you blink, you miss it," she said, then giggled. She had a sweet laugh, and Drake enjoyed listening to it. He couldn't help but smile.

Another boarder, Lizzie, wanted to know, "What are you doing this far north?" She looked truly curious.

"Looking for a change," Georgia said, but she didn't sound convincing.

Velma, the only remaining boarder, watched and listened, but didn't say a word. She dutifully ate her meal.

"That was delicious, as always," Drake said, after wiping his mouth with a napkin.

Jenny stood and cleared away the dishes. Drake pushed back his chair. "Sit down, Sheriff," their hostess said firmly. "You've been working hard all day, and the Lord knows what a terrible day you've had." She turned to Georgia then. "And you, my dear," she said gently, then carried a pile of soiled dishes to the sink.

Velma collected up more dishes and joined Jenny at the sink. The two women then busied themselves dishing up dessert. This was Drake's favorite part of the meal, and he never knew what he would end up with.

"There you are, Sheriff," Velma said, placing a bowl of hot apple pie with clotted cream in front of him.

He leaned forward and breathed in the wonderful aroma. It always reminded him of home. "Thank you, Velma. Jenny makes the best apple pie in town."

Jenny stared at him and arched an eyebrow. "Only in town?" she asked, then chuckled.

Drake loved coming here, even if Jenny did try to marry him off to whichever of the women she deemed he needed to marry that particular week. He knew it was all a game to her and played along with it. He would keep coming even if she didn't see it as a game. The food here was far better than the diner, although their food was good too. Just not quite up to Jenny's standard. Since she originally owned the diner, it wasn't surprising. She'd sold the diner some years ago, wanting to live a less hectic lifestyle.

Whether this was what she envisioned, Drake wasn't certain. He knew it was a haven for young women. If they hadn't been so far from the major towns, he was certain this house would be full to the brim. Jenny had told him, on more than one occasion, quiet was how she liked it. She'd inherited the building and the business long ago, so it was fully paid. Money wasn't a problem for her.

"How are you going there, Sheriff? There's plenty more pie if you'd like it." She took his plate and refilled it before Drake had a chance to answer.

"Thank you, Jenny. I keep telling you to call me Drake. We're practically family." It was truly how he felt. Jenny was more like an aunt to him than the owner of the boarding house. She was one of the first to welcome him to Pleasant Grove when he'd arrived. Until today, the name had certainly lived up to its name.

Today most definitely wasn't pleasant. Not for him, and certainly not for Miss Georgia Rose. She was keeping mostly to herself. Tomorrow might be better for her, but he wouldn't count on it. The carnage she'd witnessed wasn't something you got over in a hurry. It wasn't something he was used to either, not here in this town, but at his last post – it was more the norm than not. He couldn't get out of that place quick enough.

He'd been here for several years now, and hoped he was never transferred again. Today's events made him rethink that decision, but he knew it was unlikely to be repeated any time soon.

Supper was over, and Drake needed to stretch his legs. "Thank you all for a lovely evening," he said as he stood. "It's time for my rounds and evening walk."

"Fancy company?" He was taken aback when Georgia spoke. He presumed she wouldn't want to be out at night after today's wretched events. For a while, he stared at her. "Only if you don't mind," she added.

"I don't mind at all." It would be nice for a change. "As long as you don't mind tagging along for my nightly rounds. I like to make sure everyone is safe and sound before I retire for the night." The previous sheriff had started the tradition, he'd been told, so Drake had continued it. He didn't mind – it got him out and about, and ensured he got the fresh air he needed. Being stuck in the sheriff's office doing paperwork most of the time was an unfortunate part of his job. Doing nightly rounds was more of an excuse than anything else. Still, he enjoyed it.

"Do you mind waiting while I grab my coat?" She was already partway up the stairs before waiting for an answer. He liked she was confident in what she did.

"Not at all," he said. He put his own coat on while he waited.

He watched as she came back down the stairs. "Thank you for waiting," Georgia said. Once they were outside the house, she added, "I needed to get some fresh air. I feel couped up after being stuck inside all day."

He offered his arm, and she accepted. "That's the good thing about my job. Some days at least. On other occasions, I'm stuck doing paperwork all day. People think my job as a sheriff is walking around and talking to people all day. Most times, it is far from that." *Take today, for instance*, he almost said, but stopped himself in time.

She glanced up at him in the moonlight. "Thank you for today," she whispered. "I don't know what I would have done without you."

"I did nothing except rid the earth of those scum. Rory did the hard work."

She swallowed hard, and her heart thudded. "He paid the price for trying to protect me."

They'd been down that track before. She obviously still wasn't convinced. Drake stopped walking and turned to face her. "Rory would have died, regardless. Those men knew what they were doing, and they outnumbered the men on the stage. It's as simple as that. If Rory hadn't pushed you to the floor, we would be burying you as well." Her head shot up, and she glared at him. "Rory was an old man. He lived a good life, and was loved by many. We are blessed to have known him."

Drake watched as she licked her lips. They glistened in the moonlight, along with her eyes. Drake didn't know what the pull was, but he resisted the urge to reach out and caress her cheek. "School teacher, you say?" he asked instead, trying to distract himself. They walked over to the mercantile, where he rattled the door handle to ensure it was locked, and holding up his lantern, glanced through the window. All seemed well, so they moved on.

He repeated the process with the butcher shop next door. All was quiet there as well. "You wouldn't happen to have a load of books in your trunk, would you?" he asked. "That thing was mighty heavy."

She laughed, and he enjoyed the sound. "I do. Most teachers have their own supplies, and I'm no different." She put her arm through his again. "Do you have a schoolhouse here in town?"

"We do, but it's been empty for a good while now. The teacher married and could not continue teaching. We can't get anyone to come out here. That's why we are excited about you being here." Except she had no intention of staying.

She looked up at him with those big, beautiful eyes. "I'm only here for a week," she reminded him.

He patted her hand. "More's the pity. It's the children who are missing out. Most of them don't even know how to read or write. Their parents are too busy running their ranches and farms to teach their children, and those in town have businesses to run or jobs to attend."

She stopped in her tracks. "Are you saying the children of Pleasant Grove are illiterate?" Georgia sounded annoyed, but there was a touch of shock in there as well.

There was no other way to say it, so Drake blurted it out. "That's exactly what I'm saying," he said, then moved on to the next store. It wasn't long before they stood outside a small building not far from the church. "This is it." He rattled the door handle as he had everywhere else and stared through the window as he held up the lantern. It all seemed quiet.

She stared at him as though she didn't understand. "This is the schoolhouse," he said. "The townsfolk built it with their bare hands. It's such a shame to see it stand empty like this." He stared down at her then. "Still, you have no choice. You're leaving in a week."

He let his words hang in the air. Miss Georgia Rose did not answer, but her expression was thoughtful as they moved on to continue his rounds.

Chapter Four

Georgia tossed and turned all night. It would be a tragedy if the children of Pleasant Grove were illiterate because the town couldn't secure a school teacher. Especially since she was right there on the spot.

But only for a week, she reminded herself. *But it could be longer if you want it to be. After all, you have nowhere to go. Nothing specific to do.* She covered her ears from her own thoughts, knowing it was a childish thing to do.

Georgia climbed out of bed and stepped over to the window. The sun was rising, and it was beautiful. She knew what she needed to do, so why was she pushing back? Was it because the sheriff was urging her forward? Or perhaps it was because of the events of the past days? She honestly didn't know, but she knew each and every child in that town deserved an education.

She pulled on her robe and went downstairs. She always thought better over a cup of tea and hoped the water in the kettle was hot. Surely Jenny had it on the stove through the night. Moving as quietly as she could, Georgia reached the kitchen, surprised to find Jenny already there.

"Good morning, Georgia. I'm surprised to see you up and about so early after the day you had yesterday." She reached for a cup and saucer, and poured tea into it without even asking. "Bad night?" she asked as she placed the tea on the table in front of Georgia.

"Terrible. I couldn't sleep. Barely got a wink in."

Jenny studied her. "I thought as much. The black circles gave you away."

Sitting down at the table with her own cup of tea, Jenny was thoughtful. "What's got you so worried? None of the bandits survived, so there's no one to come after you."

Georgia shook her head. That hadn't even entered her mind. "It's about the children. The sheriff…"

"Is that man laying guilt on you? I should give him a piece of my mind!" She took a huge gulp of her tea. "It's not your fault we lost the last teacher. She got married and left us, you see."

"It's always a problem," Georgia said. And it was. The school board didn't allow married women to teach. But it was fine for married men. The hypocrisy of it was so frustrating.

Jenny stood and went to the oven. The aroma of freshly cooked biscuits was enticing. "It's not your problem to worry about, and the sheriff shouldn't have made it so."

"What if I stayed a little longer?" Georgia spoke without thinking. "Would that give the town time to secure another teacher after I left?"

Jenny lifted the biscuits out of the oven and onto the wooden block that sat on the countertop. "It depends on how long we're talking about. A month? Perhaps, but unlikely. A few months would give them far more time to find a replacement."

Georgia chewed her bottom lip. A few months? Was she ready to commit to that? Right now, she'd been in town less than twenty-four hours. She didn't even know if they wanted her to stay. Or how many children were involved.

Jenny sat a plateful of hot biscuits in front of her, along with a block of butter. "Help yourself," she said. "'Tis the reward for getting up with the birds." She chuckled, then went back to the stove to attend to whatever else she had cooking.

The biscuits were delicious. Probably the best she'd ever eaten. "These are heavenly," she said, and meant every word. "About the school," she took another bite. "How many children attend?"

Jenny turned to face her. "Let me see." She counted on her fingers. "Around a dozen if they all turn up. Are you seriously thinking… oh, that would be wonderful!" She did a little dance in the middle of the kitchen.

"What are you so happy about?" Mary wanted to know as she strolled into the kitchen.

"Good morning," Jenny said. "Georgia has decided to stay and take over the schoolhouse."

What? She didn't say that. Did she? "I haven't decided…"

"How wonderful," Mary said as she clapped her hands. "The parents will be very excited."

"I didn't…" She needed to intervene, and fast. She'd made no such decision. Why did she even mention it to Jenny? Georgia groaned. Now she felt obliged to stay, and who knew if they would even want her? The mayor would have to be consulted before any decisions could be made, and he may not take up her offer. Highly unlikely, but one never knew.

"Sheriff Calhoun will be pleased. Some of those kiddies have been getting up to all sorts of mischief." Jenny pierced Georgia with her gaze. Was she trying to guilt her into taking up the position? She hoped not.

Georgia took a long gulp of her tea. Right now, she needed something a little stronger. Her innocent question about the school had turned into her being pushed toward becoming the next schoolteacher, like it or not. "I'll visit the mayor later today," she said, then went back to her biscuits.

She couldn't help but notice the wide smile on Jenny's face.

Georgia stood outside the Mayor's Office after almost an hour of grueling *talks*. She was offering her services, and the man was being demanding? Had he forgotten they had no school teacher, and from what she understood, hadn't for some time?

It was frustrating. Still, she had to think of the children.

She gripped the keys to the schoolhouse as though her life depended on it. At least now she knew what lay ahead. The agreement was three months as teacher, with the option to extend the time. That depended on them both agreeing to the extension, which suited Georgia fine.

A slow smile crossed her face. Wasn't this what she wanted all along? From the moment she'd discovered there was no active school in this town, only illiterate children, her mind was on overdrive.

Every child deserved an education, and she intended to give them one. That was if they could get the children to school. After several months of no school, of sitting about being idle, how many would turn up?

Georgia was certain Sheriff Calhoun would be happy. From what Jenny said, several school-aged children were getting up to mischief. No doubt because of boredom. The townsfolk couldn't expect anything less.

Well, as of next week, that all changed. Somehow, they needed to get the word out about the school reopening. Getting the children there could be another thing altogether.

She hurried to the Sheriff's Office. The door was closed, but glancing through the window, she could see someone inside. She grabbed the handle and opened it quickly. It was no good putting this off any longer. "Good morning," she said as she opened the door. Glancing about, she couldn't see Drake. "Is the sheriff around?" she asked.

"Afraid not," Clyde told her. "He shouldn't be long, though. Can I help you with something?"

She studied him for a moment as she thought. "Perhaps. I need a list of all the families with school-aged children. The school reopens Monday, and I want every eligible child to attend." Georgia spun around as she heard laughter from behind her. "What is so funny?" The sheriff was the one who got her involved in this, and now he thought it a joke?

"For one," he said seriously, "only a few day's notice is not enough. For another, many of the families own ranches, and have been making good use of their boys being at home. You'll never get them to attend."

She pierced him with her stare and pursed her lips. "Then why did you encourage me to stay?" she demanded.

A sheepish look came over his face, which was puzzling. "I shouldn't have. But I will give you the list, and I'll even drive you to those outlying farms and ranches." He motioned for her to sit. Georgia was annoyed and didn't want to sit down. She would prefer to pace the office and rid herself of the irritation she now felt. "The majority are here in town. I'll come along and introduce you to the parents. That should help get some children to school."

"Sounds good," she said, but she wasn't sure that was the best idea. Often speaking to the parents without other influences worked best. "I'm going to need help to move my trunk to the schoolhouse." She stared at the sheriff, and then the deputy. "My books are in it, as you know."

Sheriff Calhoun grinned. "Yes, we know. That thing was mighty heavy. It took the both of us to move it."

"I have the keys, so any time that suits you both will work for me."

"I think we're both free now?" He glanced across at his deputy, who nodded. The three set out for the boarding house.

With her books settled in at the schoolhouse, the men carried the empty trunk back to the boarding house and took it upstairs to her room. Jenny accosted them both as they left. "Lunch is ready," she said. Drake looked at Clyde, who looked as clueless as he did. "You are staying," she said firmly. "I've made enough for you both."

Drake shrugged his shoulders. "Thank you, Jenny. You didn't have to."

"You need to keep your strength up. Both of you. You never know when you're going to be asked to cart a heavy trunk of books across town." She chuckled then. "Come on, food is ready and waiting."

"Thank you, Miss Jenny," Clyde said. He appeared very pleased to have been asked. *Had he never eaten there before?* Georgia guessed not. Meals there were for the boarders, not open to anyone else. Although she got the feeling Drake had eaten there a time or two. Maybe more.

Everyone sat around the table, and after they said grace, began to eat. "This is delicious," Clyde said. "I never understood why you sold the diner."

Jenny smiled tentatively. "I wanted a quieter life. The diner was constantly busy. I didn't have time for myself. This place," she motioned around her, "gives me the quiet life I craved." She seemed melancholy then. "I enjoyed the diner for a few years, though. Until it overtook my entire life."

Clyde nodded. That seemed to answer his question.

"I adore coming here," Drake said. "It's like coming home. Everyone is always welcoming."

"Of course," Jenny said, a frown on her face.

"Not everyone welcomes the law." Drake seemed disappointed then. "They forget we are merely doing our job."

The banter around the table was heartwarming, and Georgia enjoyed it. With only her mother and herself at home, it was a rare occurrence. She was always up early, so having visitors was uncommon.

These people felt more like family than her own family, which seemed strange. She barely knew them.

"Are you looking forward to your first day of school?" Lizzie asked. "I'm sure the parents will be." She chuckled then, but Georgia knew it was true. At least with those who couldn't put their children to work. The difficulty was going to be with the children who lived on ranches. Their parents were going to be hard to convince. Not only would they lose an additional pair of hands, but in some cases, they would need to take the time to bring them to town. They'd had the same problem back home when the school first opened, but it had eventually become easier.

"I certainly will," Drake interjected. "The mischief makers are becoming a real nuisance."

"Oh?" Velma said. She didn't say much, and it was rare for her to make even a slight comment like this.

"Nothing terrible, just annoying to people. Tossing bags of flour at windows, or climbing on a roof and pouring water on passersby. That sort of thing."

"There's not much we can do though," Clyde said. "Except give them a good talking to."

"The repeat offenders we toss in the cells for an hour or two." Drake grinned then. "With their parent's permission. It's not strictly allowed."

Georgia could tell from this conversation these men cared about the town and the people. It was one of the reasons she'd agreed to stay on and teach at the school. Drake wouldn't have taken her to the school, or mentioned they needed a teacher if he didn't care about the children.

When they finished eating, Jenny collected up the soiled dishes. This time Georgia helped. Her eyes opened wide at the assortment of desserts sitting on the side of the countertop. Having men folk for lunch meant she needed more, but this was going above and beyond.

There was cherry pie, as well as bread pudding, and blueberry muffins. "It won't all get eaten, but we'll have the leftovers for supper," Jenny said with a wink. The two women carried the food to the table, then distributed dessert bowls. "Help yourselves," Jenny said, placing a bowl of clotted cream on each end of the large table.

After eating his fill, Drake patted his belly. "I haven't enjoyed a meal as much since the last time I was here."

"I'm sure you said that last time you ate here," Jenny said with a laugh. "I know what you bachelors are like – you eat canned beans far too often. A home cooked meal will do you both good."

"I'm sure you're right," Drake said as he leaned back in his chair. After clearing the dishes away, Jenny placed a coffee in front of each of the men, and tea for the women.

Georgia glanced about. She felt at ease here. She felt more at home here than she did back home. She'd signed up as the schoolteacher for three months, but what would she do after that? Pleasant Grove was the sort of place you could come to visit and never leave. She wasn't sure that was right for her. Still, she would make that decision at the end of her three-month tenure.

Chapter Five

Drake spent much of the next day introducing Georgia to the parents of school-aged children, including those in outlying areas. At the farms and ranches, the mothers were pleased the school had opened up again, but the fathers were far from happy.

"I need him here," one father said gruffly. "Farmers don't need to learn readin' and writin' anyways."

"It's the law," Georgia began, then Drake motioned for her to let him deal with the man.

"Irvin," he said gently. "Don't you want Henry to have an education? He might need that in the future. Times are changing."

"Don't need no education to plow a field."

"What about your inventory? Your sales reports? Who does that?" Drake was pretty sure he knew, but asked anyway.

Irvin pushed back his well-worn hat and scratched his head. "Me foreman does it. What does it matter?" Enlightenment spread across his face as he understood where Drake was coming from. "I guess he can go to school. Just to try it out, mind. *Now,* can I get back to work?" He stormed off before Drake had a chance to answer.

"I can see why you insisted on coming along," Georgia said.

"I know these people. Besides, you wouldn't have found your way around to get to these out of the way places. You also never know who or what you might come across." She'd had one awful encounter, and Drake certainly didn't want her caught up in something like that again.

"I can't thank you enough. The school will be full on Monday."

Drake glanced down at her. The woman was far too naïve for her own good. She would be lucky if half of the children turned up, despite their parents promising they would be there. The town kids were more likely to go, but not those who lived out here. "We still have a few places to visit. Don't hold your breath for any of these. People working the land need as much help as they can get. Their children provide free help, and the boys are especially useful."

Georgia did not look happy. He didn't know how it worked where she'd lived, but that's how it worked around here. "I know, they need an education," he said before the words could leave her lips. He helped her up into the buggy, then moved on to the next place. It was going to be a long day.

~*~

Georgia looked ready to drop from exhaustion. Drake knew how she felt. It had been mentally draining trying to convince parents to allow their children back at school. It had been too long, and most of them relished having their children at home, working for free.

"I can't believe how hard that was," Georgia said as he dropped her back to the boarding house.

"Evening, Sheriff," Jenny said, as he opened the front door. "Just in time for supper."

He stared at her. "I couldn't. It's an imposition. Besides, I ate here yesterday."

She put her hands on her hips. "Nonsense! I allowed for you to be here, knowing you two were traipsing around the countryside today. How did it go, anyway?"

"As I expected, the townsfolk were on board, but not the others."

Georgia looked most unhappy. Jenny put a hand on her shoulder. "Hopefully they'll come around. But don't count on it."

"I know. It's really sad for those missing out. There's nothing I can do about it," Georgia said.

She seemed resigned now, whereas she hadn't earlier in the day. He took off his hat and placed it on the stand at the door.

"Take a seat here in the sitting room, Sheriff. Supper won't be long." Drake sat as directed. It was good to get the weight off his feet. He didn't seem to do a lot of that lately. Sitting at home at night wasn't the same as being here, surrounded by friends. He had to admit it got lonely sometimes.

A hand on his shoulder startled him. "Sorry to wake you, Sheriff," Jenny said. "Supper is ready."

It was unlike him to fall asleep like that. It had been a big day, but he still didn't expect to nap, and in someone else's home, no less. "I apologize," he started, but Jenny interrupted.

"No need to apologize. We're all friends here. We know what a hard-working man you are." She smiled then, and Drake knew there were no hard feelings. Besides, Jenny wasn't like that. She was probably the most easy-going person he knew.

They walked to the kitchen together, and she motioned him to sit down. In all the years he'd eaten at this boarding house, they'd sat in the dining room only a handful of times. The boarders had always preferred the kitchen with its more relaxed atmosphere. Jenny put on a wonderful spread for Thanksgiving and Christmas, and the dining room was used then. He'd had some wonderful memories in this place.

Drake wasn't sure what made him feel so melancholy, but he needed to heed what was going on around him. These were good people, and good people made him feel wonderful. He listened to the banter, and added his opinion here and there, but mostly he sat back and listened. His gaze seemed to gravitate to Georgia most of the time. The woman intrigued him.

"More chicken, Sheriff? Vegetables? There is plenty left." Jenny always ensured he had enough to eat.

"I've had more than my fair share already," he said. "I will have to walk it off later."

Jenny laughed, then cleared the table. Not five minutes later, she placed the desserts where the main course was previously.

"You really are spoiling me, Jenny," Drake said, and meant every word. He glanced across at the selection of desserts. At home, he had no dessert, only a main meal, and that often comprised canned beans, bacon, and eggs. He knew it wasn't the best thing to eat – he'd been told on several occasions.

"Chocolate cake?" Jenny asked, passing him a plate with an enormous slice of cake on it. She didn't wait for an answer.

"You really are spoiling me," Drake said as he accepted her offering. He'd only just begun to eat it when she placed a mug of coffee in front of him. He glanced across at Georgia, who seemed to find the entire episode funny. He guessed it was. Jenny seemed to bend over backwards to ensure his every need was met. If she wasn't at least ten years older than him, Drake might have thought Jenny was trying to win his affections.

After the dishes were done and the kitchen tidied up, they retired to the sitting room, where Drake finished his coffee. "It's been fun, ladies. Thank you, Jenny, for your kind invitation. Now I have rounds to do. Hopefully, I'll walk all this excellent food off in the process."

"If you're insinuating you're overweight, Sheriff, you are very much mistaken. You're a good-looking man, and oh my, look at those muscles." She reached over and squeezed them. The other women laughed, and Jenny turned red, suddenly dropping her hands. "Sorry, Sheriff. I don't know what came over me," she said, then hurried out of the room. Drake felt somewhat embarrassed too and hoped *his* face wasn't red.

"Goodnight everyone," he said as he put on his coat and snatched up his hat. "It's been wonderful, but I have a job to do."

They all bid him goodnight. Except for Georgia. She glanced toward him but said nothing. "Would you like to tag along, Georgia?" he asked. Her expression gave him the feeling she would.

"That would be lovely," she said, and Drake helped her into her coat.

They were both surprised when he opened the door. His hand in the air, ready to knock, was Clyde. The surprise on his face was comical. "Deputy," Drake said. "What are you doing here?" It was then he noticed the flowers in his hands.

He shoved them toward Georgia. "These are for you," he said, then stood there awkwardly. Disappointment written all over his face.

"We were just leaving," Drake said firmly.

"Um, thank you, Clyde," Georgia said as she took the flowers. She breathed in the fragrance and smiled. Suddenly she seemed disappointed too. He didn't know if that meant she was disheartened about going for a stroll with him instead of Clyde, or for some other reason.

Lizzie stepped forward. "You two go. I'll put these in a vase for you," she offered. "Are you coming inside, Deputy? It's far warmer in here."

Clyde stood aside to let them pass, then went inside himself. "Rounds," Drake told the other man, although why he did, he wasn't sure. What *he* did, and with whom, was none of Clyde's business. Then it hit him. *Was Clyde vying for Georgia's affections?* Drake couldn't be certain, but since she'd only agreed to stay for three months, he doubted she would be open to a relationship with anyone. But he couldn't say for sure.

Chapter Six

Strolling around town with Drake was nice.

Georgia was always relaxed in his company, which was confusing to her. She'd never really felt at home with men, probably because most of them had an ulterior motive — they wanted to marry her. Drake had no such aspirations. He was simply happy to be her friend.

And that suited Georgia fine.

As they strolled past the schoolhouse, she felt like she'd come home. Schools were her happy place. When she spoke to the mayor, it surprised him she only wanted a three-month contract to begin with, but after such a traumatic experience, she wasn't willing to commit to more. Now, only days after she'd arrived in town, she wondered the same thing.

The people here in Pleasant Grove were lovely. At least those she'd met so far. Drake told her there wasn't an unkind person living here, and she could believe it.

"I'll bet you can't wait to start." His voice came out of nowhere and seemed loud in the dark. It was near silent this time of night, which Georgia enjoyed.

She glanced up at him. The moonlight played across his features. Jenny was right, Drake was handsome. He was more good-looking than any other man she'd ever met before. But it was his kindness that drew her to him. "I admit I am looking forward to it. I enjoy working with children."

"They're good kids," he said. "Even those who have been getting up to mischief. There's been no school for far too long."

"I'll rid them of their boredom," she said, then laughed. They both knew that was the reason the children had been getting themselves into trouble. She was pleased to know they hadn't been involved in anything serious, like vandalism or stealing. That sort of behavior was more deep-seated and wasn't usually the result of boredom.

Drake held the lantern up to the window. "It looks fine. I can't see anything out of place." He turned to face her then. "Are you going to church tomorrow? If so, I'd like to accompany you."

Georgia smiled at the sudden change of subject. She wondered how long had he been working up to ask. "I am, and I would be very appreciative. I know few people in town. It's always hard being the newcomer."

He appeared disappointed. It made her wonder if Drake had some sort of plan to make her his own. But that was stupid. Neither one of them was interested in marriage, if she'd understood what he had been saying these past days. Not that he'd said it outright, but there were hints here and there. The marshal back home had the same philosophy. For the wife of a lawman, life was difficult.

"Are you coming?" He held the lantern out in front of himself and headed toward the next building. They were already halfway through his rounds. Georgia enjoyed Drake's rounds more each time she accompanied him. She knew it was not the rounds making her happy, but the man she was with.

The next morning, it was all hustle and bustle in the house. After breakfast, everyone hurried to get ready for church. Jenny had a lamb roast in the oven, which left the house smelling amazing.

Georgia stood in front of the mirror and checked herself over. Everything seemed to be as it should. She pulled on her bonnet, which completed her outfit. It was then she heard the front door being opened. Muffled voices followed. Her heart fluttered at the thought of Drake standing at the bottom of the stairs waiting for her, and Georgia admonished herself. She was only here for three months, and she needed to remind herself of that fact.

Not that Drake was interested in her in that way. He was merely interested in her friendship. She was acting like a silly schoolgirl, which was quite unbecoming when she was the schoolteacher.

She tied her bonnet and headed downstairs. Georgia tried to keep her eyes straight ahead, but they kept wandering toward the man waiting there for her. He looked completely different in his Sunday best. He was quite handsome in his sheriff's uniform, but dressed like this? It had her heart pounding.

"Good morning," he said, putting her off her concentration. One wrong step and she would… "Steady on," Drake said, grabbing her as she tripped coming off the bottom step. She fell against his chest, and his arms were around her. The last time they stood like this was when he helped her out of the stagecoach. She was surrounded by dead bodies then.

The thought brought her back to reality. She was blessed to have gotten out of that situation alive. She wasn't certain she'd get out of this one unscathed. Georgia pushed herself away from him and glanced up. His expression was hard to read. He didn't seem unhappy, nor did he seem pleased. "Thank you." Those simple words seemed to diffuse the confusion between them.

"Are you alright?" he asked as he fussed.

"I'm perfectly fine, thanks to you. I'm ready when you are." The others suddenly appeared, which meant they would walk as a group. The church wasn't far, but it was probably a good thing. She was developing feelings beyond friendship for Drake, and it would never do.

The thing Georgia needed to keep in the back of her mind was if she married, she lost her job. By agreeing to become the schoolteacher, she agreed to stay single. Certainly it affected her, but more important than that, it meant the children would no longer have a teacher. And that was far more significant than her own selfish needs.

The thought made her feel hollow inside. Georgia had never felt this way about any man before, but she also didn't believe Drake felt that way about her. She had to move forward and push her feelings aside.

Jenny clapping her hands brought Georgia out of her thoughts. "Looks like we're all ready. Let's go." They moved out of the boarding house and onto the street.

Georgia looked back. Merely glancing at the building evoked feelings of home for her. She'd never felt so welcomed as she did here. Drake reached for her hand and linked their arms. "Are you alright?" His voice was low, so only she could hear.

"I'm feeling a little melancholy," she said with a sigh. "I guess I miss my mother."

"But not your home?" He appeared puzzled.

Georgia shook her head. "Not my home town. It's complicated," she said as she glanced up at him. Drake nodded then, but didn't quiz her further, and Georgia was grateful for that. They walked the rest of the way to the church in silence. When they arrived, Georgia stood outside listening to the organ music. "It looks so inviting," she said, then moved forward. Drake squeezed her hand.

Once inside, he found them a place where the entire group could sit together. Georgia closed her eyes and simply listened to the organ music for a few minutes. It fed her soul. She knew this was what she needed. With everything that had happened over the past days, the peacefulness that always overtook her at church was what she needed, what her heart craved. She lifted the bible and opened it to her favorite passage, reading the words over and over in her mind.

She could feel Drake's eyes on her, and was certain he was curious about her. At this moment, she didn't feel comfortable telling him. Maybe one day, but not yet. It was her choice entirely, and she was keeping it to herself. She may never reveal – to anyone – how she was compromised and was forced to leave her beloved hometown.

Georgia swallowed back the emotion that threatened to overcome her and concentrated on the service that was about to begin. She carefully closed the bible she held in her hand. Why she hadn't brought her own bible with her today, she wasn't sure. Back at the boarding house, it was sitting on the side table next to her bed. She would make a mental note to bring it with her next week.

The bible had belonged to her dear father. When they lost him a few years earlier, Scarlett gave the bible to her. "Your father wanted you to have this," she'd said. His name was written on the front page in his own handwriting, and included the year he was born. It was a treasure to Georgia, and was something she never intended to part with.

Drake reached across and covered her hand with his. "Are you sure you're alright?" His frown showed her how much he worried.

She swallowed, then nodded. "I am, I promise," she whispered.

"Good morning, everyone," the preacher said. "And a very warm welcome to our newest parishioner, Miss Georgia Rose. For those who are not aware, Miss Rose is our new schoolteacher." He glanced across the sea of worshippers. "Where are you, Miss Rose? Please stand up so we can all see you."

Feeling the heat travel up her neck and face, Georgia reluctantly stood. Drake continued to hold her hand and squeezed it. She felt the comfort he'd intended and sat almost as quickly as she stood. She was grateful there was no applause. That would have been the absolute end. She wouldn't have coped with that at all.

"Now for the first hymn," the preacher said.

She lifted the hymn book and turned to the correct page. Not that she needed the words to sing it. This was a hymn she knew well. As the organ music began, everyone stood and then sang. Despite this, Georgia sang not a word. Her mind was in confusion, but she was certain it was the newness of her surroundings causing her to feel that way. Not to mention the work she had ahead of her. Children who hadn't been to school for most of the year was a scary thought. She did not know how many would turn up, but if she listened to Drake, it wouldn't be many. Jenny, on the other hand, felt the parents would get them there simply to have some peace for a change.

The hymn ended, and everyone sat. She followed suit. Georgia felt Drake's eyes on her. The preacher began his sermon, and she had to concentrate to understand the message. It wasn't him; it was her. She suddenly felt unwell. The walls seemed to close in on her.

Georgia stood and fled the church. She heard the gasps behind her, but could do nothing about it. She had to get outside to the fresh air. *What was wrong with her?* She sat on the wooden bench outside the church hall. Gravel crunched, and she glanced up. Drake was heading toward her, a concerned look on his face.

Chapter Seven

Drake couldn't believe how relieved he was to see Georgia sitting outside on the wooden bench.

She was taking deep breaths, and she was deathly pale. He sat beside her. "What's going on?" he asked gently.

"I'll be fine," she said, trying to brush it off. "I just felt… unwell."

It wasn't long before another parishioner joined them. "Doc," Drake said, surprised. "What are you doing out here?"

"Come to check on the patient." He raised his eyebrows as though daring anyone to challenge his assessment. "You are white as a ghost, Miss Rose. Let me check you over."

Georgia glanced about. Drake could almost read her thoughts. He was certain she would think, *Out here?*

"Let's move into the hall," the doc said. "There is plenty of time before the service is over. Drake, bring her a glass of water, please."

He hurried ahead, and the doc took Georgia inside. They went to the back of the room, and Drake was at the front, in the kitchen. It meant he couldn't hear the conversation, but that was probably the point. Out of respect, he took his time with the water, standing outside the kitchen until he was called closer.

After a few minutes, Doc Higgins motioned for him to approach. "I think it's delayed shock," he said quietly, taking the water from the sheriff.

"After all this time?" Drake was confused. He thought shock happened immediately.

"It can happen. It's unusual, but I never discount it." He turned back to Georgia then. "You need to rest for the next few days. Take it easy."

"School begins tomorrow," she said firmly. "I am not putting that off."

Doc ran a hand through his hair. "I hate to say it, but I doubt you'll have any students there tomorrow. Of course I could be wrong."

"I will ensure she rests today, Doc," Drake said firmly as he sat down next to her. "Does that mean sleep, or just not doing anything?" He studied Georgia as he spoke. She was fuming, which meant he wasn't going to be popular with her. It might give Clyde a way to take over.

He shook himself mentally. Neither of them had a chance, since she was leaving in three months. Drake couldn't see Georgia letting herself get attached to anyone when she knew she was leaving. He certainly didn't want *his* heart broken.

What was he thinking? He didn't want to get married either!

"Am I allowed to stay for a while to meet everyone?" Her voice was quiet and seemed meek. It proved to Drake how unwell she really was. He could kick himself – he had picked she was unwell on the way here. Why didn't he convince her to stay home?

"It's my fault," he blurted out. "I could see she was ill, and should have insisted Georgia stay home."

Doc chuckled. "How do you think that would have worked out?"

Even Georgia laughed. "You tried, remember? I didn't think I was bad enough to stay home. Please don't blame yourself."

He shoved his hat further back on his head. Right now, he felt frustration and annoyance at himself. A good friend would be attuned to their friend's needs. Even if they hadn't known them for very long.

Low murmurings began. "Guess we're about to have company," Drake said. "Are you sure you want to stay?"

"I'm certain," Georgia said.

Doc patted her back, then left them alone.

It wasn't long before Jenny and the other boarders surrounded them. They were concerned, which he could understand. "Doc says she had to rest for a few days."

"I'll rest this afternoon, but that's it," she said stubbornly. "What the doc doesn't know won't hurt him."

"But it might hurt you," Jenny said firmly. "Oh, by the way, Sheriff, I meant to invite you for lunch."

Again? he wanted to say but refrained. "If you're certain," he said instead. Lately, it felt almost like he lived there. Not that he was complaining.

"Lamb roast – your favorite."

Georgia laughed. "It seems everything is Drake's favorite."

"It's called food," Jenny answered. "Anything that can be eaten is the sheriff's favorite."

They all laughed, and then Drake and Jenny left for the church kitchen. He grabbed a tea for Georgia, and a coffee for himself.

"I think the sheriff likes you," he heard Lizzie say to Georgia as he approached. He pretended not to hear. He decided if that's what she thought, perhaps he was not trying hard enough to only be Georgia's friend. He should keep his distance more, but would ensure she was well before doing so. He'd promised the Doc.

He handed her the tea and a biscuit, then backed off, leaving the women alone to chat. He mingled and talked to the other parishioners, but his heart felt hollow. After today, Drake vowed to keep his distance from the charming school marm. The last thing he wanted was to fall for her, only to have her leave, never to be seen again.

Merely thinking about it made his heart ache.

By the time they began the walk home, Georgia appeared somewhat better. She had a little color in her cheeks again, and didn't look quite as fragile as she had earlier. She was talking and laughing and seemed to be back to her old self.

Still, he'd promised the doc, and Drake never broke his promises. Now to get her to comply.

"I'm sorry I ruined things today," she said quietly.

He studied her. "What did you ruin? You were unwell. Are still unwell, and need to rest like the doc said."

She waved a hand across in front of herself. "I don't need rest. I'm fine now."

He continued to study her. "What if you become unwell again, faint in front of the children? What then?"

Georgia stared at the ground, then lifted her head and glanced at him. "I won't," she said firmly as she glared at him. Her features were taut, and Drake could see she was stressed. He patted her hand.

"Everything will be alright," he said. "You just need time. Like the doc said, you went through a traumatic experience. Something most folks never experience."

Her bottom lip quivered, but it was clear she would not let herself cry. She'd done that when he'd got her out of the stagecoach. The moment she'd seen the carnage surrounding them, after the immediate shock had gone, her emotions took over. As much as he hated seeing women cry, that was exactly what he wanted her to do right now. Drake knew she would feel better.

Suddenly, she rolled her shoulders and straightened her back. "It's not the first time I've experienced trauma," she said firmly. He wasn't sure if she was trying to convince him or herself.

"Do you want to talk about it?" He wouldn't push the issue, but if she needed to get it off her chest, he was ready to listen.

"Not here, not now." She glanced about at the group they had tagging along. "Perhaps never."

It was then Drake remembered his vow to back off, to keep his distance. He now wished he'd never made that promise to himself. Still, he needed to protect his heart at all costs.

Drake opened the gate to the boarding house and let the ladies in ahead of him. Jenny stepped forward and unlocked the door. Everyone moved inside. He helped Georgia out of her coat and removed his own.

"Now you must sit and rest," he said firmly. He watched as her lips pursed and her hackles went up.

"What the sheriff meant," Jenny said quietly, "was that you will feel better if you sit for a while and put your feet up." She threw him a look that could freeze hell.

As Jenny left the room, she shoved him toward the kitchen. "You'll attract more flies with honey than vinegar," she said harshly.

He stared at her blankly. "I do not know what that means," he said, feeling totally confused.

Jenny sighed. "It means don't tell her what to do. Make suggestions, don't try to force Georgia into resting, because it simply won't work."

"I've noticed how stubborn she can be," he said.

Jenny rolled her eyes. "Just go back in there and sit down. Talk to her. That should keep her in the chair for a bit."

Drake ran a hand across his chin. He wasn't good at keeping people entertained. That had been proven time and again. Sure, he was fine with some small talk, but after a while, he did not know what to say. It made him wonder how long he could keep Georgia confined to the sitting room. "What should I talk about?"

"Give me strength," Jenny said, then headed toward the oven. Drake shrugged his shoulders then returned to the sitting room.

"What did you think of the service today?" he asked. Then his heart thudded. She probably heard fifteen minutes of it, if that.

"What I heard was good," she said. "The preacher seems nice."

"Preacher Howard is nice. He's always available to listen or to talk if you need it."

She screwed up her face, and Drake knew he'd put his foot in it. She'd already told him she wasn't ready to talk, so why did he have to bring it up again? Small talk. It's what he was supposed to do, right? Only it didn't feel right. "Do you need any help tomorrow?" Despite doc's orders, she was determined to go, so he might as well help if he could.

"Lunch is ready," Jenny said, and Drake reached out to help Georgia out of her chair.

Her expression was fierce. "I'm not an invalid," she ground out. Then she closed her eyes. It was only for a moment, but it seemed to calm her. "I'm sorry," she said, then took his hands. "I'm not used to being fussed over."

He felt awkward for a moment or two, but nodded and clasped her arm through his, then led her into the kitchen. "It smells amazing in here," Drake said, and meant every word. He led Georgia to the table, and once he had her seated, sat down beside her. Jenny and Mary placed the food in the center of the beautifully set table, then they all joined hands.

Jenny waited for a heartbeat before saying the prayer. "Thank you, Lord, for this food, and these friends. Thank you also for sending us a new teacher for the children. Please help her heal so she can do the thing she does best. Amen."

Echoes of *Amen* could be heard around the table.

"You can let go now," Georgia said as she glanced at their entwined hands. Drake looked down. *What if he didn't want to let go? What then?* A smile crossed her lips, and it made him smile, too. So much for keeping his distance.

As he had done every other time he'd eaten there, Drake passed the heavy platter around the table. The ladies seemed to appreciate it. Even if they didn't, Drake was more than grateful to be invited to this friendly home. It felt like a proper home to him, despite the rotation of guests from time to time. Most of the boarders were long term, but some, like Georgia, only stayed a short time. Although now she would be there for at least another three months.

The thought warmed his heart.

When everyone had their plates filled, Drake sat back down and piled food onto his own plate. He took a mouthful. It was delicious. Georgia reached out and placed the gravy jug in front of him. "You forgot this," she whispered.

He reached out to lift it, and his hands brushed against hers. Warmth filled him, and Drake was confused. For a moment, he froze and didn't know what to do. But deep down, he knew what he had to do. He just didn't want to do it.

How did you distance yourself from someone who had become more than a friend in such a short time? A person you would lay down your life for? He'd done that before he'd even met Georgia, and he would do it again. In a heartbeat.

This was the thing he'd tried to avoid, but circumstances had him spending more time with her than he'd planned. Drake wasn't sure what he should do now. He promised the doc he would ensure she rested today. He could pass that responsibility over to Jenny, and he was certain she would gladly accept, but was it what he wanted? How would Georgia feel being discarded as though she didn't matter?

The trouble was, she did matter. She mattered greatly to him, and truth be told, he wanted to spend more time with her, not less.

"Would you like more, Sheriff?" Jenny's voice cut through his musings, and just as well. His mind was bringing up all sorts of scenarios that he didn't want to think about.

"Thank you, but I couldn't eat another bite," he said, rubbing his belly.

Jenny laughed. "You could always loosen your belt." Everyone at the table laughed, and he chuckled along with them. These people were family. He enjoyed coming here, and it wasn't just for the food. "I hope you've left room for dessert." Jenny smiled, and he knew she was still joking on his behalf.

He couldn't help but grin. "There is *always* room for dessert! That will never change," Drake said, then handed his empty plate to Jenny at her silent request.

Mary and Jenny worked quietly to clear the table and refill it with culinary delights. His mouth was salivating at the delicious flavors he was about to indulge in. "Apple pie with clotted cream," Jenny said. It was always the same on Sundays. She had a routine meal for Sunday lunch, but he wasn't complaining. "There's also a custard pie, and I made orange muffins as well."

"Thank you, Jenny. You've been busy, and I'm sure we all appreciate it." Drake knew he did and was certain the others sitting at the table did as well.

Georgia turned and smiled at him, then reached out and squeezed his hand. He would survive the next three months, he was certain. It was after that, when she left, that already had his heart ripping into two.

Chapter Eight

Georgia couldn't believe it was the first day of school.

The walk to the schoolhouse was invigorating. She felt as though she had a whole new lease on life. Whether that was because it was the first day, not only for her, but for her students, she wasn't sure.

She didn't believe it was her enforced day of rest only yesterday. Drake had hung around all day, ensuring she rested. They chatted some of the time, but she could tell he wasn't used to socializing much. Small talk seemed to be quite a burden to him. Jenny and the others spent much of the day in the sitting room with them. At one point, they moved out into the back garden and took in the fresh air. It was so peaceful sitting out there sipping tea. Georgia could see herself living here long term, but had no intention of committing to that just yet.

When she arrived at the schoolhouse, two students were waiting outside. She remembered them from the other day when she and Drake informed the parents the school was reopening. These girls were local; their parents owned stores in town.

Outwardly, she smiled. Inwardly, her heart pounded in anticipation. How many other students would turn up today? "Good morning, Laura, good morning, Daisy," Georgia said. She turned the key in the door and motioned them inside. "Since you two are the first to arrive, you may choose your desks." The girls let out a yelp and turned to each other, then hugged.

They both ran toward the desks. "Walking please ladies," Georgia said firmly, and they slowed down.

"Yes, Miss Rose," Daisy said.

"Sorry, Miss Rose," Laura told her. Then they both sat at their chosen desks.

Georgia handed each child a slate, then added a slate to each of the remaining desks. She wondered if it was wishful thinking others would be along soon. According to Drake, she was lucky to have two children turn up today. It was still early, so more may yet arrive.

It was a beautiful fall day, and although it was a little chilly, Georgia didn't believe she needed to light the fire. The girls seemed comfortable enough so decided against it.

She studied the writing on the blackboard. By all accounts it had been there for some time. The lettering the previous teacher had added was perfect, so she had no thought to remove it.

"Miss Rose," Daisy called out. "We have a visitor."

She spun around, hoping it would be another student. Instead, it was the sheriff. He looked quite imposing standing there in the doorway. His height meant he almost hit the top of the doorway, and his bulk filled the door almost completely. Drake was a big man, but she hadn't realized how large he really was until now.

"Oh! Good morning, Sheriff," she said, trying to fight back the smile that came to her lips. The last thing Georgia wanted was to appear enthusiastic to see him. "How may I help you?"

Drake pulled his hat from his head. "Good morning, Miss Rose," he said, being more formal than she expected, but with children there, it was understandable. "I was walking by and decided to check if you need anything. Good morning, girls," he added.

Georgia handed each of the girls a book. "You can both read, can't you?"

"Yes, Miss Rose," they said in unison.

"We're the best readers in the class," Daisy said. They both giggled.

Georgia sighed. These two wanted to have fun. She wanted to teach. No matter what, she would have to work with what she had.

"Good. Open the book and read chapter one while I speak with the sheriff." She moved to the doorway, where Drake stood tall and proud. "Is everything alright?" she whispered.

"That's my question. I wanted to ensure everything was fine with you. One or two of the boys can be a bit… boisterous, I guess. Looks like an easy first day. I'll leave you to it." He reached out and squeezed her hand, and Georgia's heart fluttered. She wanted to pull her hand away. At the same time, she didn't.

He turned and headed out, then suddenly turned back. "I'll pick you up after school? Walk you home?"

Georgia chuckled. "I believe I can find my own way home."

Drake nodded. "I'll collect you, anyway." And then he was gone. Georgia stood watching him momentarily, but turned back to the chants of her students.

"Miss Rose has a boyfriend, Miss Rose has a boyfriend." The girls giggled and chanted at the same time. Georgia knew if she didn't put a stop to it, these two would take over her classroom.

"Girls!" she demanded. "Stop this immediately. You are meant to be reading the first chapter." Her words were firm. She needed her students to understand who was in charge, and it wasn't them.

"Sorry, Miss Rose." Again in unison, and they bent their heads as if to say they meant it. If they hadn't been quietly chuckling, she might even have believed them.

"Do I need to split you two up?" Georgia heard their collective gasp.

"No, Miss Rose!" They sounded appalled, but at least she got the message across. It was going to be a long day, but also, hopefully, a good one.

Once the pair had finished reading the chapter, there was a discussion about the story. There was no point in them reading if they didn't understand what they'd just read. Thankfully, they both understood the story and the message behind it. With that session over, they moved onto sums, which they did on the slates Georgia had previously distributed.

By now, she felt exhausted. Was it because these two were full of mischief, or was it because of her shock? At least according to Doc Higgins it was shock, but she really did not know if that diagnosis was correct.

"It is time for lunch yet, Miss Rose?" Daisy wailed. "I'm starving!"

Georgia gazed at her sternly. "Young ladies are not starving, they are hungry. Daisy," she said firmly, "from now on, you will speak clearly and in an acceptable manner. You will not wail or carry on the way you did moments ago. Is that understood?"

Daisy nodded, then her attention turned to the doorway. Georgia wondered who was there now. Couldn't the townsfolk leave her alone?

"He *is* her boyfriend," Laura whispered loudly.

"Laura! Enough of that nonsense. Outside for lunch, you two. And behave yourselves!" She turned back toward Drake to see him grinning. He tried to hide it behind his hand, but his smile was far too wide for that to happen.

"You're not helping," Georgia ground out.

"Bit of a handful, are they?" He chuckled then, and Georgia was not impressed.

She pulled her own lunch out of her bag and pushed past him to sit on the step outside. "Have you eaten?" She opened the package that held two sandwiches. "I'll never eat all this." She glanced across at Drake, then rolled her eyes. "This is Jenny's doing, right? And the reason you're here. I should have known. That woman, as lovely as she is… well, she's trying to match us. Isn't she?"

He laughed as he reached for half a sandwich. "She instructed me to be here for lunch and said she'd packed my lunch with yours." He took a bite. "This is good," he said. "To answer your question, yes. I'm certain she's trying to match us."

Georgia frowned. "She can forget it. I will be gone in three months."

It was Drake's turn to frown. "I thought that was still up in the air." He took another bite.

She shrugged her shoulders. "I have no idea either way. No matter who it is, there's no point trying to match me up with anyone. If I decide to leave, then I will. It's far better not to have any attachments. Besides, if I found someone special, I'd lose my job if I married." Drake knew all about that. He'd told her it was the reason they lost the last school teacher.

One thing she knew – the children of this town deserved to have a teacher who was consistent. Someone who would be here for at least three months. Preferably for several years. Whether or not that was Georgia was a totally different question.

"If that's lunch, I guess we've had it," Drake told her as he wiped his mouth with the napkin. "Jenny thought of everything."

"The muffins were delicious. I didn't expect any of this. She balked when I said I was making lunch. Now I know why."

Drake studied her before speaking. "It wasn't so bad, was it, sharing your lunch break with me?

Sharing your meal with me?" He raised his eyebrows and Georgia wasn't sure what to make of it.

Her words had been matter-of-fact, and she could see how he could take offence at them. Georgia packed up the lunch pail and stood. "Time for you to go. Girls, lunchtime is over."

They both groaned, but went back inside.

"I'll be back after school," Drake said. He leaned in, and she thought he was going to kiss her, but whispered in her ear instead. "I miss you already," he said, but immediately appeared dismayed at having said the words.

If that were true, he was right to feel that way. Georgia did not want a relationship, not with anyone. Her life was complicated. Not to mention the fact she'd be compromised by a hideous man in the worst possible way. In view of many.

She couldn't get the humiliation out of her head. After she'd screamed, several men came running. Instead of saving her from that awful man, they stood there gawking as he clutched her breast. Two men even smirked. As she continued to fight Sherman off, they still stared and did nothing to help her. Until her mother came outside to find out what the commotion was all about. It was only then Sherman let her go. Scarlet strolled up to him and slapped his face. She'll never forget the expression on his face.

Despite all that, instead of Sherman being punished for assaulting her, Georgia felt the wrath of the townsfolk, and the mayor sacked Georgia from her beloved teaching position. It was as though the entire situation was her fault, which it wasn't.

With Drake gone, and only two students, the room seemed empty. She continued regardless. "We will now practice our times tables," she said, and was met with a groan. "Now girls, I'll have none of that." Georgia pointed to a place on the blackboard. It was then the chanting began.

She smiled. Every child needed to be able to recite the times tables. It would get them through until the end of their days.

Chapter Nine

With her arm linked through Drake's, they strolled back to the boarding house. Georgia surely wouldn't deny she was tired. She looked exhausted. "I'm still not convinced you should have opened the school today," he told her. Drake wasn't sure what sort of reception he would get. It was very apparent she didn't like being told what to do.

"I won't deny it. I am tired." She turned to him and smiled briefly. "It was to be expected. New environment, new students, and an enormous challenge. Without a teacher for such a long time, the students were… difficult."

He frowned then. "You want me to talk to them?"

She pierced him with her gaze. "I most certainly do not! What sort of teacher would I be if I needed the sheriff to pull them into line? No, you keep your distance." She faltered then and chewed briefly on her bottom lip. "Please mind your own business."

Drake wanted to laugh out loud. He'd never had anyone tell him to mind his own business before. Especially not someone so petite as Georgia. She certainly was a force to be reckoned with. No wonder she was a wonderful teacher. He couldn't imagine her students trying to cross her in the classroom. Or anywhere, for that matter.

"Here we are," he said as he knocked on the front door.

He watched as Georgia glanced around. "It's so pretty here," she said, sounding quite melancholy. "My mother has a garden like this, only far bigger." She leaned down and breathed in the fragrance of the colorful flowers surrounding her.

"It is lovely. Makes you feel relaxed just looking at it." It was true. Whenever Drake visited, calmness came over him. Still, he wasn't sure if it was the garden or the building, but he was pretty sure it was more the people.

Jenny opened the door to them. "Right on time," she said. "Supper will be ready shortly. Both of you sit down and rest until then."

Drake stared at her. "I couldn't," he said firmly. "It feels like I've had practically every meal here for close to a week."

A slow smile crossed Jenny's face. "Is there something wrong with that? Haven't you enjoyed the food? What about the company?" She pierced him with her gaze and moved her eyes between Drake and Georgia. He suddenly realized what was going on. Jenny was up to her match-making ways, and he was caught in the middle - again.

Any other time, he wouldn't be upset about being matched with Georgia. The problem was, she was leaving town in a few months. At least, she thought she was. What if she changed her plans and stayed? If she told him right now she would be here for the duration, would that change things for him? For them?

He was certain it would, but the truth of the matter was, she had made no such announcement. Which meant he had to protect his heart. "Thank you, Jenny," he said firmly, "but I must decline. I have… paperwork to complete." Without another word, he turned around and left the boarding house.

He heard Jenny call his name, but Drake reluctantly ignored her. As he walked toward the sheriff's office, he felt the pangs of regret. He knew exactly why he'd refused Jenny's invitation, but on thinking it over, realized the sheer stupidity of it. There was no reason he and Georgia couldn't be friends, except he wanted more. Far more.

As he walked into the office, he noticed Clyde sitting at his desk. "All quiet?" he asked.

"All quiet," Clyde told him.

He didn't even bother removing his hat. "Then I'll be off. You know where to find me if you need me."

Clyde studied him. "At the boarding house?"

Drake shook his head. "Not tonight. I'm eating at home."

"What happened with…" Clyde suddenly stopped. Was he thinking of going after Georgia for himself? If so, Drake wouldn't stop him. He couldn't even if he tried. Georgia was a free spirit, and it was up to her to decide if she was willing to be courted.

He didn't respond to the deputy's half asked question, but left the room as though Clyde hadn't spoken. How he went forward from there, he wasn't sure. Losing his friendship with the young woman would be a tragedy. They got on so well. Apart from being her friend, he felt like her protector, even if she didn't appreciate it.

Perhaps tomorrow he would pop into the schoolhouse and check on her. He wondered how many children would turn up. If he were in the same situation, Drake was certain the lack of support would frustrate him. Perhaps tomorrow would yield a better result. For Georgia's sake, he hoped so.

Drake pulled the frying pan out of the cupboard with a clatter. He had two eggs and three slices of bacon left. Plus two slices of bread, which he would toast. It was a far cry from whatever Jenny had made for him to enjoy.

As he stared down into the hot pan, he thought about what a fool he was. These past days spent with Georgia, even those where he had fleeting time with her, had been his most enjoyable. Why would he refuse to accept an offer to spend even more time with her?

The answer was simple – he was a fool.

A little after nine and Drake had completed his morning rounds. He stood across the road from the little schoolhouse. Inside was Georgia Rose, but fool that he was, he had distanced himself from her. As he stared at the building, the doors suddenly opened, and several children ran outside, slates in their hands. They wandered around in pairs, glancing down at the ground. Now and then they stopped, bent down, then scribbled something on the slate. They then moved on and repeated the process.

It had Drake curious. What were they doing?

Suddenly, it was as though the rest of the world had stopped. Miss Georgia Rose stood at the top of the schoolhouse steps. She watched over her young charges, a smile on her face. He had kept his distance for two whole days. It felt more like a year.

Suddenly she glanced his way, and Drake wasn't sure what to do. He froze for close to a minute, then tipped his hat to her and walked away without a word. He resisted the urge to look back over his shoulder to see if she was watching him, but instead, slipped into the diner. He'd be able to see the schoolhouse from there.

"Sheriff!" a female voice said, and he spun around at the unexpected interruption. "So nice to see you. What can I do for you?"

He forced himself to smile. "Good morning, Meg. I haven't dropped by for a while, and thought I'd check how you were doing." It was only a half-truth, but he had been telling himself for ages he needed to check on her.

"Can I get you something? A coffee and muffin?" The petite widow studied him then. "Did you have breakfast today? You look to be losing weight." She grabbed for his shirt and moved it about. "I was right. You sit down and I'll be back shortly." Drake didn't move. He felt like he was in a daze. Meg pulled out a chair and sat him down. "I won't be long," she said.

He had a perfect view of Georgia from here and continued to watch her. Even to his own mind, it was the wrong thing to do. He forced his gaze away.

"There you go," Meg said. "On the house."

"Oh, I couldn't," Drake said, as he glanced at her.

"Yes, you can. You do far too much for this little town. Now eat up before it goes cold." For the first time, he glanced down at the plate. It was full to the brim with sausages, beans, scrambled eggs, and two hot biscuits on the side. He glanced up at Meg as she set a mug of coffee in front of him.

"Thank you," he said, feeling more grateful now than he had before – when he was in a daze. When he glanced up again, Georgia and the children were gone. Likely back inside the schoolhouse.

Meg returned once he'd finished eating. "What were you watching?" she asked gently as she took his soiled dishes.

He gazed at her. Meg was far more perceptive than he'd given her credit for. She followed his line of sight. "Oh," she said before he could answer. "The schoolhouse. It's that pretty new schoolteacher, isn't it?" Drake wasn't sure what to say. Did he tell her he had a soft spot for Georgia? Or did he keep quiet? "What are you doing about it?" she asked before he had a chance to say anything.

"I…" He shrugged his shoulders. "Nothing. She has only committed to three months. After that," he shrugged again, "she will probably be gone."

"And you," Meg said, covering his hand, "will be left with a broken heart. Am I right?"

She knew him far too well.

"One thing I've learned in life," Meg said gently, "is to go after what you want. Otherwise, it will be too late." She squeezed his hand then. "Or do you want Clyde to win her heart instead?" Meg raised her eyebrows at him.

"What do you mean?"

"I saw Clyde last night with a box of candies. He appeared to be heading toward the boarding house."

"That low-down," Drake stopped. Apart from the fact he was in the company of a lady, he had no hold over Georgia.

Meg raised her eyebrows again. "I assume that means you would like to pursue our new schoolteacher."

Drake scowled. "I would, but then she might lose her job." It was a two-pronged problem.

"One problem at a time." Meg patted his hand. "The way I see it, you need to find out if she likes you. If she does, you'll sort out the other problem between you."

Without another word, Meg stood, taking the soiled dishes to the kitchen. Drake sat watching the schoolhouse for another few minutes before he left. Meg's words rolled over in his mind, and he knew he had to take a stand. If he had to fight Clyde for Georgia's affections, so be it.

Chapter Ten

Georgia sat in the window seat in the sitting room, watching the activity outside. She was supposed to be reading.

There was little going on at this hour of the night, but she hoped to get a glimpse of Drake. Even a small one. It had been days since she'd set eyes on him, although she was convinced she'd felt his presence earlier in the day at the schoolhouse, but when she glanced up, he wasn't there. It was the strangest thing.

She'd missed him these past days, and wondered what she'd done to keep him away. She'd grown to look on him as more than a friend, but truth be known, Drake didn't see her the same way.

Georgia knew she should have stuck to her beliefs – men were not worth the time of day. That had always been her philosophy back home, but there were none worth worrying about. She sighed, then went back to reading her book.

The knock at the door a few minutes later startled her.

When she opened the door, it surprised Georgia to see two men standing there, scowling at each other.

Clyde stood to the right with a box of candy, and Drake stood to the left, also with a box of candy. More than anything, she was confused.

Drake shoved the candy box toward her and pushed his way inside. He closed the door before Clyde could get inside. "What are you doing?" Georgia asked, annoyed at his behavior, then opened the door to the deputy. "Take a seat, Clyde, and I'll call Lizzie for you." She glared at Drake. "You can sit down too." She purposely tried to sound flippant. He was acting suspiciously like a jealous boyfriend.

Georgia went upstairs and knocked on Lizzie's door. "Clyde is here for you," she called through the door.

"I'll be right there," Lizzie said, excitement filling her voice. It wasn't long before the door was flung open and Lizzie raced down the stairs. They were still embraced in a hug when she returned to the sitting room. Drake had an incredulous look on his face, and Georgia couldn't work out why.

Then it hit her.

"These are for you," he said, pushing the box of candy toward her again. He had a sheepish expression on his face, and her beliefs were confirmed. He'd believed Clyde was pursuing *her*, not Lizzie.

"Thank you," Georgia said, pursing her lips, "but I'm not sure I want them." Her hands on her hips, Georgia tapped her foot. "I know what you were thinking, and I don't like it. Not one bit."

"I'm sorry," he said, pushing the box of candies toward her again. This time, she accepted them.

"Supper is ready," Jenny called from the kitchen doorway. She did a double-take when she saw Drake. "Are you staying?" she asked, her manner a little cold. It was obvious to Georgia that Jenny was irritated with Drake for staying away. He had ruined her match-making plans, there was no doubt. Then a slow smiled crossed her lips. "Of course you are," she said. "There's plenty to go around."

He glanced from Jenny to Georgia. He appeared conflicted.

"Come on, then," Jenny said firmly, urging him to stay. She seated Lizzie and Clyde together, and Georgia and Drake. She didn't mind, but Drake needed a change of attitude. All he needed to do was talk to her.

After everyone was seated and they said grace, everyone filled their plates. "How is school going?" Drake asked. He wasn't his usual self. Tonight he seemed… stifled? It was like he was afraid to say much.

"School is excellent. There are more children attending now."

"I noticed a couple of boys earlier today." So he was there – she was certain he was. "I was doing rounds, and you all went outside. I was surprised to see Henry and William there. I was certain they would be made to work on their parent's property."

"Martha and Clara are attending as well. We are a class of six now. Hopefully that will grow over time."

"You can't force these things." He went back to eating the beef stew on his plate. Georgia had missed Drake tremendously over the past days. Although she knew Drake had missed Jenny's home cooking during his absence. She had to wonder if it was the food or her he'd really come for.

"We missed you, Drake," Jenny said, as though she had read Georgia's thoughts.

He glanced up. "I missed coming here. Missed everyone. Don't take this the wrong way," he said firmly, "but I missed Georgia more than the rest of you." He chuckled then, and Jenny's smile seemed to almost crack her face open.

It had been a pleasant evening, made better by Drake's unexpected appearance. They opted for a stroll around town afterwards, including his nightly rounds. Georgia didn't mind, provided she got to spend time with Drake.

The moonlight mostly lit their way. Drake also carried a lantern to help him see inside each building. When they arrived at the schoolhouse, he turned to her. "What were the children doing outside this morning? They appeared to be foraging."

"They were. The lesson was about appreciating nature. Each pair had to find a plant, then they each had to write something about it. Little did they know it was really a way for me to assess their writing skills."

He grinned. "Not just a pretty face," he said, reaching out. He placed the lantern on the ground and cupped her face with his hands. "I have fallen in love with you, Georgia," he said. "But I worry about my heart."

She stared at him. "I've fallen for you as well."

He studied her. Was he surprised at her declaration of love? Was he so naïve he didn't know she felt that way? "What is this about your heart?" she asked, suddenly realizing what he'd said.

His hands dropped from her face and he glanced down at the ground. He kicked at the stones there like a love-struck teenager. "Drake? Talk to me." It was like pulling hen's teeth. Or dealing with one of her students. "I don't understand."

He glanced up from his feet and studied her. "When you leave in three months, I'm not sure I can survive. These past days," he cupped her cheeks again as he stared into her eyes. "My heart felt as though it was being pulled in different directions." He leaned in and brushed her lips with his own.

The brief kiss wasn't enough. Georgia reached up and put her arms around his neck, and pulled him down to her. She kissed him deeply. At first he seemed surprised, then he submitted to her silent request. When she finally pulled back, Georgia rested her head on his chest. "What's this about me leaving in three months?" She glanced up into his face. He couldn't hide his confusion if he tried.

"Your contract is for three months and then you're leaving?" He seemed suddenly uncertain.

Georgia lifted a hand and caressed his cheek. "That was the original plan. Before you stole my heart," she said, then rested her head on his chest again. Standing there with him, she felt more content that she had for a very long time.

Drake's hands were suddenly on her shoulders, and he stepped back. He stared down into her face. "Georgia," he said, looking very solemn. "May I court you with the prospect of marriage?" He appeared terrified, but also sincere.

Georgia knew it was now or never. She had to explain her difficult situation to Drake. The thought had her fighting back tears. She wiped at her eyes, then confessed. "Drake, there is something I need to tell you." He gazed at her. "I am not the person you think I am. Back home, I was…" She closed her eyes tightly, then opened them again. "I was compromised," she finished quickly. His expression didn't change, even when Georgia gave him all the details.

"It wasn't your fault, and praise the Lord, you came out virtually unscathed. I love you, and always will," he said, pulling her close again.

Tears filled her eyes. It was the happiest moment of her life so far, but Georgia was certain the days and years ahead would bring far more happy moments.

Almost three months had passed, and the town was filled with excitement. The sheriff and the schoolteacher were getting married.

They had sought permission for Georgia to stay on as the school teacher until they could find a replacement. Or until she found she was in the family way – whichever came first.

The ladies at the boarding house, including Lizzie, helped with her wedding gown. It was to become Lizzie's wedding gown in a few week's time. Clyde had popped the question just days ago. Georgia wondered whether Mary and Velma would end up married. Or Jenny. She might be past a so-called marriageable age, but she was still a woman, and still able to bear children.

Jenny may not agree unless she met the right man, but Georgia could picture her with her very own family. The woman was a nurturer. She should have her own husband and children to spend time with and spoil.

Scarlet had arrived two days ago for the wedding. Drake collected her from Pine Creek. He didn't want to risk Georgia's mother being harmed on her way to their wedding. She'd stayed at the boarding house since then. She drove everyone crazy with her airs and other nonsense, but despite that, they all adored her.

Georgia took a deep breath. Was this really happening?

With all the petite buttons at the back of the gown secured, matching shoes on her feet, and a bouquet of fresh flowers from Jenny's beautiful garden, it was time to make her way to the church.

"Something borrowed," Jenny said, handing Georgia a garter. "It was to be for my wedding many years ago. Let me help," she said, her voice almost breaking. "A stray bullet killed my man just days before the wedding," she said, answering the silent question hanging in the room.

"Oh Jenny, I'm so sorry," Georgia said. "I will take so much care of this. Thank you."

"Something blue," Lizzie said, handing her a blue ribbon for her hair.

She leaned in and kissed Georgia's cheek. "Thank you," Georgia whispered.

Then Scarlet stepped forward. "Something new," she said, putting a shiny new necklace around Georgia's neck. "I love you so much, and your groom is a wonderful man. I hope he makes you as happy as your father made me." She wiped a stray tear from her eye as she leaned in to hug her daughter.

Georgia was momentarily speechless, then as she hugged her mother, whispered, "I love you. I only wish Father was here today." They both shed a tear or two.

When they all had their emotions under control, it was time to leave.

It wasn't very far, and Georgia had decided to walk. The women left as a group. She looked over her shoulder at the boarding house she had called home for the past three months. What a delightful time she had enjoyed there.

After the ceremony, it would no longer be her home, but Georgia knew she would always be welcomed there. From today, she would live in the sheriff's cottage. She felt sure they would outgrow it fairly quickly. A year or so down the track, and she hoped the pitter patter of little feet would fill their home.

Mary and Velma ran ahead and opened the church doors for them. "Are you ready?" Jenny asked, as they stood in the doorway.

She glanced toward the front of the church. Drake stood proudly in his Sunday best, looking even more handsome than normal. Clyde stood by his side, acting as his best man. Their positions would be reversed when Lizzie and Clyde married in this same church in less than a month.

Lizzie stood by her side, looking resplendent in her bridesmaid's dress. It was really her Sunday best, but it worked for this auspicious occasion. On her other side, Jenny had brought a new ensemble. She was giving the bride away in tandem with Scarlet, and decided a mother-of-the-bride outfit was in order.

Lizzie stepped ahead of them. "Is everyone ready?" she whispered as she glanced over her shoulder.

Georgia took a deep breath and let it out slowly. "I think so," she said, then straightened her shoulders and stood tall. "Yes, yes, I am."

With Scarlet on one side, and Jenny on the other, they began the slow trek down the aisle. The organ music played, and Drake turned to face her, his expression one of pure love. Georgia's heart fluttered. This amazing man was about to become her husband. She wondered what life would bring, but knew their days together would be wonderful.

Epilogue

Three years later…

"Honestly, Georgia," Drake said. "I wish you would stop fiddling with that vegetable garden." Two-year-old Robert sat on his father's knee. "You come and hold Robert, and I'll do that." She could surely see his frustration?

Eleven-month-old Ella chose that very moment to wail. Holding Robert under his arm, he went to tend to Ella, who had been napping. His least favorite thing to do was changing diapers. Especially smelly, soiled diapers. He was doing the best he could to help his wife, who was very pregnant.

They had outgrown the sheriff's cottage a long time ago, and moved into their own home on the outskirts of town. Scarlet loved Pleasant Grove and the boarding house so much, she moved in, despite their offer for her to live with them.

"Look who I found," Drake said, carrying Ella under one arm and Robert under the other.

Glancing up from tending her garden, Georgia smiled. "You won't be able to do that when there are three. Or more," she said, raising her eyebrows.

Drake put the children to the ground, then went to Georgia, who was struggling to stand. "Here, sit and rest," he said, guiding her into the chair he'd occupied a short time ago. "You look pale. Perhaps a nap is in order."

"Don't fuss. This is baby number three. It's not like I'm not used to being pregnant." She rolled her eyes, and Drake realized she was frustrated waiting for this baby to appear.

He reached for the pitcher of water and poured a portion into a glass. "Drink this. You look dreadful. I'm going for the doc."

Georgia took the water, but waved off his concerns. "Honestly, I'm perfectly fine. I still have a few days at least."

It was Drake's turn to roll his eyes. A few days and she wanted to do manual labor. Or perhaps that was the reason she wanted to do it. He'd heard doing heavy work could bring on the birth. Not always, but sometimes. Well, now he was a wake up to her scheme, he'd make sure Georgia rested more. She needed to be fully alert and have all her wits about when the baby made an appearance.

"No doc," she insisted. "I would like to rest, though."

Relieved his wife was finally listening to reason, Drake again helped Georgia to her feet. They were walking from the garden and through the kitchen, heading toward the bedroom when it happened. "Mama wet herself," Robert said, looking very concerned for his mama.

At almost the same moment, there was a knock at the door. "Hopefully that's the doc," Drake said, sitting her down at the kitchen table. "Thank goodness you're here," he said, opening the door quickly, but not even looking at who was there.

Scarlet and Jenny stood in the doorway gawking at him. He called them his two mothers-in-law. Most men had only one to deal with, but Jenny was his self-appointed second mother-in-law.

"Georgia's water broke," he said in a panic. "I need to get the doc." He was pacing the room and distressing the children.

"Sit down!" Jenny demanded. "Now take a deep breath." Her hand on his shoulder, Drake was already feeling more calm. "You used to be a sheriff. How can you be so panicked about a baby about to arrive?"

He glanced up at her. She was right. "This is different," he said. "I'm alright now. I'll get the doc."

Jenny studied him. Was she assessing if he was in a fit state to get Doc Higgins and bring him back here? "Are you certain you are capable of that?" She was watching him closely, and he almost squirmed under her gaze.

"Of course," he said firmly, then stood. "Provided you and Scarlet will be here with Georgia and the children."

"We will," she said. "Now get out of here. That baby could arrive at any moment."

Drake dashed outside and took more deep breaths. He'd done this twice before, so why he was so panicked, he did not know. Or perhaps he did. The first two births went perfectly. What were the odds the third birth would go as well?

He couldn't bear the thought of losing his beautiful wife. Or their children growing up without a mother. His life hadn't been the same since she arrived in Pleasant Grove. Until that time, he was simply going through the motions. Drake had thought he lived a full and happy life, but he was wrong.

When Georgia arrived, despite those first rough days she endured, he knew he'd found his soulmate. Denying his own feelings was the worst thing he could ever have done. If it hadn't been for Meg at the diner, he would have lost her forever.

It set in motion a lot of life changes, including Mary, from Jenny's boarding house, training to be a teacher. Georgia was able to supervise her until she was ready to teach. The school was now full of activity, and the town owed that to Georgia for getting it running again.

"Drake? Drake!" Doc almost yelled his name. He was woolgathering while waiting for the door to be answered.

Drake shook himself, trying to focus. "Baby's coming," he said between trying to catch his breath. "Georgia's water has broken."

Doc Higgins snatched up his medical bag and hurried out the door. Drake followed behind, still somewhat breathless. "Any contractions?" Doc asked.

"I didn't think to ask." This was baby number three. He knew the basics, so why didn't he check? Drake already knew the answer – he wanted to get Georgia medical treatment as quickly as he could.

They arrived at the front door, but Drake hesitated. "Doc," he asked before the other man could go inside. "Is she going to survive this?"

Doc sighed. "If I have any say in it, she will. Your wife is in safe hands."

"I know, Doc. I know." Still, it wouldn't hurt to say a prayer or two.

The waiting was pure torture, but sitting in his most loved setting, the boarding house, made the unbearable easier to bear. Most of the time, he'd kept silent due to worry, but now and then he chatted with the new sheriff.

"You would have seen a lot in your years as a sheriff," Drake said. He'd seen a lot himself, and he was a junior compared to this man. Far older than Drake, but around Jenny's age, he seemed trustworthy, and was very personable.

"I have. Far more than you, I'm certain. It's a good thing you got out when you did. Married men are not good lawmen," Sheriff Ralph Darcy told him. "All I want now is a quiet life." The fact he had consumed many meals there already was not lost on anyone. Especially not Drake.

It seemed like hours later when Scarlet arrived back at the boarding house to tell Drake, and anyone else who cared to listen, a healthy baby boy had arrived. Drake couldn't get to his feet fast enough. He'd drank enough coffee to last a lifetime, and despite his love of cake, had not consumed even one bite.

"How is Georgia doing? She is alright, isn't she?" He almost ran back home, and couldn't get there quick enough. He shoved the door open and heard the click of the doc's medical bag as he approached the bedroom. "Doc," he said as he let out an enormous sigh of relief. Georgia was sitting up in the bed, cradling their newborn.

"Bed rest for your wife, and I better not hear otherwise." He grinned then. Doc knew Drake would follow his instructions to the letter. He loved Georgia with all his heart and would not do anything to harm her.

"Thank you, Doc. I give you my word." He moved toward the bed as the doc saw himself out. That feeling of elation never left him, even after all this time, and their three children. Drake leaned in and kissed Georgia's forehead, then outstretched his hand to their son. Baby Thomas quickly grabbed at his father, his little hand curling around one of Drake's fingers. "He's beautiful," Drake said quietly, and kissed his wife again, this time with a brief kiss to her lips. "Thank you for this amazing gift."

He sat on the side of the bed and stared at the two of them. How he got so lucky he would never know. If he hadn't slipped into the diner that day, would he be sitting here now? Drake would never know, but he was certain fate had played a huge part. They were meant to be from that very first meeting, despite how traumatic it must have been for Georgia. Without it, they may never have met. He may never have held her, and he would never have known divine intervention was at play.

He took his newborn son in his arms as Georgia's eyes fluttered closed. Scarlet came in and took the baby from him as he made his wife comfortable and pulled up the bedding to keep her warm. Together, he and Scarlet went to the sitting room to introduce Thomas Calhoun to his big brother and sister. If he had his way, there would be many more Calhoun's to come. That decision was not his, and would come from the Almighty himself.

From the Author

Thank you so much for reading my book – I hope you enjoyed it.

I would greatly appreciate you leaving a review where you purchased, even if it is only a one-liner. It helps to have my books more visible!

Cheryl Wright

About the Author

Multi-published, award-winning and bestselling author Cheryl Wright, former secretary, debt collector, account manager, writing coach, and shopping tour hostess, loves reading.

She writes both historical and contemporary western romance, as well as romantic suspense.

She lives in Melbourne, Australia, and is married with two adult children and has six grandchildren, and twin great-grandchildren.

When she's not writing, she can be found in her craft room making greeting cards.

Links

Website: *http://www.cheryl-wright.com/*

Facebook Reader Group:
https://www.facebook.com/groups/cherylwrightaut hor/

Join My Newsletter:

https://cheryl-wright.com/newsletter/
(and receive a free book)

www.ingramcontent.com/pod-product-compliance
Lightning Source LLC
Chambersburg PA
CBHW070629120726
47909CB00004B/1371